MAGGIE'S GOLDEN MOMENT

By Cynthia Profilet
Illustrated by Ann Barron
CCP Sterling Press

Maggie's Golden Moment © 2005
by Cynthia Cain Profilet

Library of Congress
Catalog Card Number: 2005908323

ISBN 0-9637735-1-8

Published by
CCP Sterling Press
6811 Old Canton Road #3802
Ridgeland, Mississippi 39157

Illustrated by
Ann Barron
Jackson, MS

Art and Design Director
Josh Hailey Studio Inc.
JoshHaileyStudio.com

Printed and bound by
Friesens
Book Manufacturers
Louisville, KY

Printed in Canada

Looking Back, Moving Forward
A tribute to the storm victims of Hurricane Katrina, 2005

In Maggie's Golden Moment, author Cynthia Profilet pays tender tribute to the courage and fortitude of a young girl with challenges to overcome. Maggie's journey is no easy one. Her past is fraught with obstacles and setbacks. Yet because someone is willing to step out and believe in her, Maggie perseveres and finds the friends for whom her heart has been longing.

Like Maggie, the children of the Gulf Coast Region are now facing challenges that, at first glance, appear insurmountable. These children and their families need friends more than ever. With the help of friends, the storm victims can prevail over adversity, ceasing to be victims at all and becoming instead the victors we know them to be. All it takes is a friend, and that friend can be found in each of us.

-Sheila Fox Lotterhos
Editor "VISTE Volunteer"
St. Augustine, FL

For "Mr. Jordan"
Director of Bands
Canton, Mississippi
1953-1965

Thank you to the "Music Man" who planted the
joy of music in my heart for a lifetime
of appreciation, integrity, and success.

The many lives you touched are greatly
enriched simply because you shared your
gift with us.

- Cynthia Cain Profilet (1955-1963)

Author's Note:

Maggie's Golden Moment is for all of us who have broken the rules, gotten caught, and, in spite of ourselves, prevailed. This young girl pulls at our heart-strings as few characters can. The message is one of

Hope
Faith
and
Love.

Maggie's Golden Moment

Cynthia Cain Profilet
Illustrated by Ann Barron

*For Donna —
a Tri Delt
Girl Is like
a melody...

May God
Bless You With
many GOLDEN!
MOMENTS!"*

*May 11
- 2006 -*

*Peace and
ΔΔΔ Love —
Cynthia Cain Profilet*

School: First Day of Spring

Ms. Profi stood and stared as each bundle of energy exploded into her classroom. The second grade – a first for Ms. Profi. The children were so young, so small, not like the seventh and eighth graders she had taught for years.

The first day of spring meant squeaky new tennis shoes, starched shirts, pants and dresses. Wide-eyed, the kids studied the teacher, each other, and the classroom. They were quiet, still.

"RRIIINNNGGG!!" the bell screamed.

In their desks. Time for work.

The teacher began, "Welcome. I am your new substitute. My name is Ms. Profi. I will call the roll. Please stay...."

Suddenly, a flash of colors tore through the room,

"Wait! Wait! Stop, teacher!" My name is Maggie," the child stated, hands on hips, backpack falling off shoulders.

"Maggie, in your desk - RIGHT NOW,

the one closest to the bulletin board!"

"P-p-please, Ms. Profi, not by me," Satasha stammered.

The others grumbled along, "Not me. Not by me. Not me."

Maggie protested, "Teacher, they're picking on me."

Class began. Small groups of students moved to their learning stations.

"Ouch! Stop that, Maggie. Give me my paper. Ms. Profi, Maggie just broke my colors. Please make Maggie move. She's mean," Michelle cried out.

Without a word, Ms. Profi stared at Maggie and pointed to the vacant desk in the corner. Maggie flashed her angry eyes at the girl.

Golden Moments

Within a few days, Ms. Profi had moved Maggie to every single seat in her classroom. Not one student wanted to sit by Maggie.

One day, Maggie was very quiet, and she moved very slowly.

At lunch, Maggie sat alone. Ms. Profi watched the young girl as she ate her sandwich. The teacher saw light in Maggie. With eyes closed, she lowered her head. Then she shook her head. "Maggie needs help," Ms. Profi thought to herself . "What can I do to help her? There must be a way to reach Maggie?" Ms. Profi imagined.

Each day Ms. Profi talked with the class about being kind to others, having good manners and caring about others. She spoke of love, peace, and joy.

This was the best part of the day for Maggie. She listened very closely.

One day, Ms. Profi talked about Golden Moments. "The best ones happen when you least expect them. They happen quickly, but the memories last forever. A moment that is an answer to a prayer."

Maggie's bottom lip began to quiver as she heard the message of hope in Ms. Profi's voice. "Maybe there is an answer to my prayer," the little girl whispered.

The Letter

After several days' talks, Maggie wrote notes to Ms. Profi. They were hand delivered. She usually wrote a note when the other children were busy. Slipping out of her desk, on her tip-toes she put the folded paper into Ms. Profi's hands.

Ms. Profi unfolded the paper. She read the note over and over. Softly, she said to herself, "Maybe there is hope. Maybe..."

The next morning Maggie walked over to Ms. Profi's desk. "Did you get my note?" she asked Ms. Profi.

"Yes, Maggie I did. Thank you," the teacher smiled.

Hope - Maybe ?

Maggie minded her "p's and q's" all morning. In fact, no one complained about her at all.

By lunchtime, Ms. Profi approached the young girl. "Maggie, you may be the leader of the lunch line to the cafeteria." Maggie carefully led her class to lunch without any trouble.

With her very best manners, she ate her lunch very quietly. No trouble.

After lunch, Ms. Profi read a story to the class. She read the story of the "The Velveteen Rabbit."

"The little boy had..."she read aloud. Little heads nodded as they struggled to stay awake. They needed a nap before time to play.

Soon it was recess. Maggie played under the mighty oak.

No
one
came
close
to
her.

Ms. Profi took a deep breath and walked slowly toward Maggie. "Maggie, look at the daffodils. Mmmm – Don't they smell sweet? When the wind blows, the daffodils lean in the same direction. But they don't bend nor break because together they are strong. If one daffodil had to stand alone against the wind, it would break. But daffodils stick together. Friendship is like that. Without friends, you have no one to lean on," the teacher spoke softly.

"Ms. Profi, look. The daffodils. The sunshine makes them gold!" Maggie was amazed.

"Very good, Maggie, like the daffodils, friendship is golden."

Maggie's face lit up, and for the first time all year, she smiled at her teacher as the wind lifted her pig-tails and tossed them about in all directions.

"OWWW! Ouch! Let go, Maggie."
Kate rose to her feet from her desk.
    Maggie held on tightly to Kate's
pig-tail. She giggled with delight.
She gave the little girl's hair one last
twist and settled back in her desk.

"Maggie! Time out! Not one more peep out of you. Do you hear me? Let's step into the hall." Ms. Profi said sternly.

The rest of the class sat in silence. Maybe they would hear what the teacher said. "Shh, shh, shh," the students repeated until the room fell silent.

Friendship is Golden

Ms. Profi towered over Maggie as they stood in the hall. Maggie trembled with fear.

"Teacher! T-te-teacher, p-p-please don't stop helping me. You are very kind. You are my only friend. P-p-please, I'll be good. I'll be your helper. I promise."

"Maggie, you do not pull hair in my classroom!" Ms. Profi said.

Maggie fired back, "I didn't, I didn't do..."

"Maggie, stop!"

Maggie's mouth closed, and her eyes opened – wide!

Ms. Profi said, "Good, Maggie. Thank you for not interrupting me."

Lowering her voice, Ms. Profi looked into Maggie's sad, hopeless eyes. She wanted to encourage this confused, precious little girl to be all that she could be. "Maggie, remember, friendship is golden. Treat others the way you want to be treated. Now, let's go back into the classroom. I want you to apologize to anyone that you have hurt. You can start with me!"

"I'm sorry, Ms. Profi," Maggie sighed.

Finally, Ms. Profi and Maggie returned to class. Tears of joy were in Maggie's eyes. The teacher's face was radiant.

"Maggie, tell the class what you just learned," said Ms. Profi.

Maggie said, "Friendship is golden... If I am kind to others, they will be kind to me. I want to be kind to others. I want a lot of new friends. No more being bad. I will be good. I am sorry.

~SILENCE~
and
a
smile
from
the
class

A Prayer Answered

The children arrived at school the next day. They all shouted at once, "Look! Look! Ms. Profi, at the door!"

Ms. Profi looked toward the door. Maggie was all dressed up in a white taffeta dress! Her eyes were as shiny as her fancy shoes, and her smile was as splendid as her dress.

"I went to church with my Aunti," Maggie burst forth. I said my prayers, too! **God bless my new friends and my teacher**. I brought a golden daffodil for each one of my new friends."

Carefully, Maggie
tiptoed around the
room and placed
a golden daffodil
in each one of her
friend's hands. Very
slowly, she returned
to her desk by the
door. Suddenly, the
class clapped and
cheered for Maggie.
The look in her eyes
softened. She was
beginning a new
journey. It was one
that would lead to
love and friendship
- and this was what
Maggie needed
most.

Like the daffodils

friendship is golden